Sausage Patty

By
Diane Allevato

Illustrated by Trish Van den Bergh

A Grant from The William and Charlotte Parks Foundation
makes this book possible

Sausage Patty
By Diane Allevato

Published by Animal Place

Printed in the United States of America

ISBN 0-9644062-1-7

$3.99 soft cover

All proceeds/profits from the sale of this book
are donated toward the care of animals living at Animal Place

Design by Anagrafx Advertising-Design

1

Where Am I?

Saturday, January 18

I am not happy. Delete that . . . I am wretched. It is Saturday afternoon and it is raining. Delete that . . . the sky is leaking and the world is doomed. It is the middle of winter and there are buds on bushes and leaves on trees and it is 64 degrees. We moved from New York and it is like we crossed some barrier into the Weird Zone.

I am sitting at the computer making the first entry into my TRANSITION JOURNAL. How miserable do I have to be to voluntarily start on one of Father's recommended projects for the New Year? Transition Journal . . . more like a Diary of Despair.

How could this happen? Six weeks ago I was happy, as in having friends and living in Manhattan. I was in 8th grade, one semester from graduation. *The Scramblers Yearbook for '96*: There I am on page 15. Sydney Landcom, Honor Society, Vice-President

DICT

. . . Film Critic's Circle, President . . . Sound & Sense, Editor . . . "Never at a loss for words," "Let's go to the movies!" Nickname: Matinee.

Then Father came home one night with a list, and the destruction of my life was Item 4. My Father is a financial analyst, which means he is a very strange man. He analyzes everything. He outlines problems and makes lists and plots the end of my childhood. If only he wasn't my only living parent, but he is. There is no going to Mom for help. My mother is dead. I am a half-orphan. In New York it was no big deal. Everybody knew that Mom died three years ago. I didn't have to answer stupid questions about it, and I didn't have to explain my father. I mean, how can you explain a guy who writes down guests' names, prominent features and personality traits after a party and who leaves you an agenda for the day next to a glass of orange juice every morning? This man charts my grades, and does spreadsheets of my allowance. I don't remember if he was a problem before Mom died, but he is definitely one now.

It is Saturday afternoon and it is raining. I have no friends, my father is driving me crazy, and my agenda reads, BUY A RAINCOAT.

Monday, January 27

This Monday looked like last Monday. I go to school. Two people tell me I talk funny and I eat lunch alone.

Tuesday, January 28

Mr. Gambi, my English teacher, said, out loud in second period that my essay was "thoughtful, literate and mature." He gave me a special reading assignment because I have already read *Oliver*

Twist. Now I will be lucky to get out of the 8th grade alive. Back home I was planning to go to Arts & Letters High in the fall. I was normal. I had friends. Here I am an outsider . . . an escapee from Manhattan living in a town with only one movie theater. I talk funny and I have read all the assigned books.

There was one bright moment today . . . Juan Merida. He is in Mrs. Grill's 8th grade home room. I watched him at lunch today. He is tall with dark curly hair and even darker eyes.

Thursday, January 30

Juan Merida . . . He comes into the cafeteria alone and sits alone for about 3 minutes. Suddenly a silent alarm goes off and a flock of 7th and 8th grade girls gets up and casually flies by his table. The bold ones drop like gulls into the seats around him, filling the table with chattering and squawking. He looks miserable. Miserable but cute . . . seriously cute.

Saturday, February 1

Father hired a part-time housekeeper yesterday. Mrs. Neufeldt's homemaking skills exceed mine . . . she can do the laundry, make pesto pasta, and smile all at the same time. While filling the house with the smell of fresh basil, she listened to Father give me some tips on cheerfulness. She rolled her eyes. I laughed. I think that was the first time I have laughed since we arrived in Sonoma, California.

Monday, February 3

I learned from listening in on the squawking in the girls' bathroom that Juan is new too. He started East Sonoma Jr. High in November and has been a social mystery. I think this means he is tall, dark, handsome, smart and inaccessible to the fluttering of many feathers. How come a new boy who is different is "interesting," while a new girl who is different is just different? I wonder if he feels like me? Out of sync and on the wrong channel.

Wednesday, February 5

I thought about interviewing for an opening on *Two Roads*, the school poetry review, but at the last minute I changed my mind. I don't know why. Everything seems harder here.

I smiled at Juan in the lunchroom today. He smiled back.

2

Tofu

Friday, February 14

A very good ending to a very bad week. I owe it to tofu. Tonight was the Parent Potluck at school. Father had to work late, so I went without a parent. I felt strange going alone, but I figured it was a toss up between feeling weird because I was alone and feeling weird because Father was there counting the fat grams in the casseroles.

I didn't want to take any risks and actually cook something. I figured going alone was risky enough. I bought corn chips and three kinds of dip. I dumped the dips into matching blue bowls and garnished them with cilantro. They looked homemade.

I got to school just in time and put out my contribution without too much attention. At least, so I thought.

"Yes, chips and dip!" Juan said as he came up behind me and scooped piles of black bean, chili bean, and tomato salsa on his paper plate. "I was afraid I might only get to eat my own

PARENT POTLUCK

concoction."

"What do you mean?" I laughed. "Some of these dishes look interesting enough. They may even be food."

"Well, they don't qualify as edible. I'm a vegan." he answered softly.

"There are all sorts of vegetarian dishes here," I said. "Macaroni and cheese, lasagna, and I think that's a broccoli quiche, or maybe it's just a greenish pie."

Juan laughed and suddenly I didn't feel like a lonely outcast. "I'm a vegan . . . a really strict vegetarian. I don't eat eggs or cheese or milk or . . ." he started to explain.

"Ice cream!" I gasped.

"Yep, no ice cream either. There are substitutes, unfortunately not on that dessert table," he moaned, pointing to the crowded rows of pies, cakes and puddings.

"Why are you a vegan?" I asked, wondering about a world without ice cream.

"I just like animals too much to eat one or to feel comfortable with their being exploited." Juan's grin was softer now. "Except for school potlucks, I don't starve. But thanks to you I can eat my tofu curry with chips and dip as an appetizer."

"Did you make the tofu curry?" I asked incredulously.

"I did. My mother is a great cook and she is really supportive of my diet, but if I want tofu, I have to make it myself." He munched his way through a second plate of my dips.

"I understand her position," I laughed. "If you won't turn me in to the home economics teacher, I'll confess that those dips came from the corner store and that I have never eaten tofu."

I sat with Juan and his parents and ate tofu curry and chocolate cake. The tofu was OK.

3

Friends

Saturday, February 15

Juan came by the house today and met Father. All went well. Juan held up under Father's heavy questioning, and I spent the day at the Merida's house. House doesn't actually describe it.

More later.

Saturday, March 1

It has been two weeks since my last entry. There is so much to write about. I wish there was someone who could do it for me. I have been very busy.

Juan and I started walking to school together right after the potluck. He lives about half a mile down the road. After school I help him with his algebra problems and he corrects my Spanish grammar. He is incredible! God, I hate girls who gush and giggle about guys. I want to be rational, but in addition to being very cute, he is also very smart. However, he can't figure out why girls hang around his lunch table and locker. He says that they don't know him, so they can't possibly like him. I told him it was because he's one of only three 8th grade boys over 5'6". I didn't say anything about his eyes and his smile.

The flock of girls almost pecked my eyes out when we started eating lunch and hanging out together, but they flew off after a couple of days. Two girls in my American history class, Melissa and Carmel, cornered me in the hall and asked about Juan. Then they asked me about living in New York City and music and stuff. I have this feeling that my social sticker price went up when Juan and I became friends.

Juan is my friend. Melissa and Carmel are my friends, too. And Jack, well . . . by association and coincidence, I may get a horse.

Sunday, March 2

It started at the Merida's place two weeks ago. Juan's family lives on a hillside ranch just down the road. It could just as easily be across the solar system. Mr. Merida is a writer and Mrs. Merida is an artist and the ranch is home to all sorts of animals.

There are chickens, ducks, llamas, cats, horses and Beans. Mr. Merida, who laughs a lot, says he feeds the chickens and ducks every morning for inspiration. Mrs. Merida says the llamas she rescued from an auction yard are to remind them of the highlands of Peru. They left Peru — or escaped Peru — four years ago after Mr. Merida wrote a magazine article that made an army general mad. When Mr. Merida talks about "soldados" (soldiers) his voice is angry but his eyes are sad. I think he does most of the talking in the family, because Mrs. Merida is quiet like Juan.

There is a quiet craziness to the entire place. There are books

everywhere, not just on shelves. There are piles of magazines in four different languages. Classical music drifts out into the yard, and chickens sort of cluck along. Cats sleep in the sun, and a dozen jars of solar tea brew simultaneously. It would put my father over the edge.

Beans is Juan's dog. He is a white border collie type dog with brown patches and brown eyes that are always watching Juan. Beans was a stray that wandered onto the Merida's place within days of their arrival in November. Smart dog! They named him Lima after the capital of Peru, but at the veterinarian's office they thought it was Lima, like the beans. So Beans it is. He is so loyal and funny . . . two orphaned ducklings think Beans is their mother and they follow him around. He is very patient but when he has had enough duck-sitting he jumps over the fence or up on the picnic table to nap in peace.

I felt like I was a spectator at a carnival of creatures. I never had any pets. Dogs were difficult in the City, and Father is allergic to cats. Mother loved animals. When I was little we would talk sometimes about a weekend place in the country where we could keep chickens and raise vegetables. It was one of those things that never happened.

And the best . . . the horses. I never touched a horse in my life until two weeks ago, and that very day I rode a horse over Sumpter Ridge to Beyer's Lake with Juan and Mrs. Merida. The whole world changes when you sit on top of a horse. Of course, you have to stay on top. A horse's muzzle is like velvet, and a horse's lips are like butterflies as they flutter around your hand looking for sugar.

Juan and I spent last Sunday just wandering over the green hills with Beans. We talked. I have moved once and my life is in pieces. He has never stopped moving . . . from Peru to Costa Rica to Boston to Los Angeles to Sonoma . . . making and losing friends at every stop. His parents promised that this was the last move until he finished high school. I told him that my father has a 5-year California plan.

We agreed, laughing, on a high school graduation friendship pact.

His mother and father talk to me too, as if I were a person . . . We talk about books, nature, music and politics . . . not just about my posture and my school work. I think they are glad that Juan has a friend. I feel like I have made a whole family of friends.

It's after 11:00 p.m., so I have to shut down. I guess keeping a journal was one of Father's better ideas. It is like talking to a trusted but invisible old friend. Oops, I forgot to write about Jack. Details about Jack, the horse . . . my horse . . . tomorrow.

4

A Proposal

Monday, March 3

I had a great riding lesson at Tumbleweed Stables today. Jack was in a good mood and he put up with my mistakes. Jack is my riding partner. He is the horse. Jack is a bay gelding. Bay is a color pattern; his body is crayon brown and his mane and tail are black. He is 10-years-old and spirited and patient at the same time. He moves like the Black Stallion in Walter Farley's book . . . like living liquid.

The first day I visited the Merida's and met their horses, I knew I wanted to learn how to ride. Pretty weird for a girl who grew up in NYC! The next day I talked to Melissa and Carmel about it and they invited me to the Tumbleweed Stables where they take riding lessons. It was like the law of polarity . . . you say something out loud and it happens. After three lessons, Gloria, the trainer, says I show real "promise". She says I have a natural seat and an affinity.

Father is supportive. He says equestrian sports attract the "right kind" of people and I can make contacts. I don't think he means Jack, but he bought me breeches, boots and a helmet without doing a cost-benefit analysis.

The trouble is now I want to buy Jack. I need my own horse in order to ride every day, and I have to ride every day to be good. If I can practice regularly, I can show with Melissa and Carmel this summer in novice classes. Of course, Juan is right: working with Jack and becoming real partners is the important thing, but being a part of the horse show circuit with the girls at the stable would be fun too.

Tomorrow night Father gets home early and I will be ready for him.

Tuesday, March 4

$500 . . . $500 . . . 500 . . . $500. Let's see if the law of polarity works with money. I wonder if the tooth fairy carries that kind of money . . . I could take out one of those back teeth I never seem to use and no one sees.

The pasta dinner with garlic bread did not work its usual magic. Father ate dinner with gusto, but before I could serve the strawberry gelato he asked me what I wanted. Actually, he asked "How much is this delicious daughter-cooked meal going to cost me?"

"Just one thousand dollars!" I answered, maybe a bit too quickly.

"Well, I guess I'll skip dessert and we can settle for a $10.00 advance on your allowance," he snorted just as quickly.

So, I explained the whole thing to him, carefully, in detail, the way he likes. Jack was for sale for $1,000.00. He was worth three times that amount, but his original owner had moved to England

and did not feel it was kind to ship and quarantine a horse. She wanted Jack to have a good caretaker rather than go to the highest bidder, so Gloria had been keeping her eye out for someone "right." Jack was a bargain and would appreciate in value 300% the minute we bought him. Father nodded appreciatively.

I explained that boarding and veterinary bills along with lessons would cost $250 a month, but I would permanently give up piano lessons, cancel magazine subscriptions, use the library instead of the bookstore, disconnect the on-line service, make dinner every Tuesday night and work at the stables 6 hours a week to cover these ongoing costs.

Father scribbled numbers on his napkin and hummed. I explained how the $1,000 capital investment would come from my college trust fund. He raised his eyebrows, stopped scribbling, and I knew I was losing ground.

"Mother left me the money for my education. What better education than to learn to do something very well. She loved horses. She used to read me the Farley horse books and she. . . " I blurted out, and then I almost started to cry. It was awful. I swallowed twice and blinked and coughed and just barely saved myself from humiliation.

Thank God Father was erasing some of the numbers and didn't seem to notice. I just want Jack so bad. Then Father put his offer on the table.

"OK, Syd. Here is the deal. I will match every dollar you earn 2 to 1. I will give you $500 to buy the horse if you earn the other $500. The money will come from your college fund because you are right, I think your mother would concur that it is an appropriate use of the funds."

Then he swallowed twice, blinked and coughed.

$500 . . . $500 . . . $5,000 . . . $50,000 . . . $500,000 . . . it may as well be $5 million dollars.

5

The Project

Saturday, March 8

I went to a winter 4-H horse show at the fairgrounds with Melissa and Carmel today. It was incredible! The pageantry is like a medieval jousting tournament . . . horses, colors, music . . . I closed my eyes and saw Jack and I stepping into the ring and the announcer calling out, "and the blue ribbon in the novice pleasure riding class to Tumbleweed's Jackstraws, a 10-year-old bay thoroughbred, ridden by Number 27, Miss Syd Landcom."

Friday, March 14

I checked with my counselor's office at school Friday about getting a job and got a 10 minute lecture on child labor laws. Unless it is informal, like working for boarding costs at the stable or babysitting, kids can't work. Thirteen is not a good age to be looking for a job that pays $500 a week or $500 a summer. I set aside $5 from this week's allowance, so I will settle for $495.

I got an A on my English composition. I wonder if I could trade it in for a B and $10.

Saturday, March 15

I went to 4-H with Melissa and Carmel. The 4 Hs stand for head, heart, hands and health . . . covering all the bases. The meeting starts with a pledge "My head to clearer thinking, my heart to greater loyalty, my hands to larger service, my health to better living for my club, my community, my country and my world."

At first I thought it was kind of nerdy but the meeting was fun! I was never a Girl Scout or Campfire Girl but 4-H isn't organized like scouting. There is a lot of activity, and the group leaders, Harold and Harriet Gribbs, are energetic. They made the meeting interesting with stories and jokes. They seemed to really care about kids becoming involved in and successfully completing their projects. The idea is to learn by doing: photography, auto mechanics, raising animals . . . . I guess I will learn to be an equestrian, but I haven't decided exactly what my project will be . . . maybe one where there is a $500 or $495 payoff at the end.

Sunday, March 16

What is wrong with me? I read the entire *4-H Projects Handbook* and nothing clicked . . . . Then the clicks start in the middle of the night. I need a project that earns me money. I can raise an animal, sell it at the fair in July, and make the money I need to buy Jack! I just have to persuade Gloria to put Jack on hold for me, persuade Dad to let me keep my project animal in the shed next to the garage, and then raise whatever kind of animal is most profitable.

Yes, yes, yes!!!!

Monday, March 17

Father was convinced. He even seemed amused. He asked if it was going to be like the spider song where the woman swallowed the cat to catch the rat to catch the spider to catch the fly. But I told him that I planned to stop at a sheep, pig or cow to buy a horse. He said that if the numbers crunched, I was free to raise anything smaller than a buffalo.

Juan was not convinced. He asked me how could I raise an animal and then sell it to be slaughtered for food. I told him that whatever it is, it isn't going to be like Beans or Jack. It's going to be a food animal. It's a project. I will raise it following all the 4-H guidelines for housing, nutrition and veterinary care. In midsummer I will show it and sell it at the fair. And will be $500 richer!

Anyway, it is hypocritical to eat hamburgers, bacon and fried chicken but not be involved with where your food comes from, and I have no intention of giving up hamburgers.

He agreed that it was hypocritical and sort of shrugged. I asked if he thought I was a horrible person or something and he smiled and said "Syd, you are something."

MEAT
IS MURDER

6

Patty

Saturday, March 22

Decisions are sometimes made for you; circumstances just helped me decide that my 4-H project will be a pig. Juan and I visited Pini's Feed Mill to research what I would need to raise different kinds of animals. There was an awful squealing and snorting going on in a pen in the rear of the store. I couldn't believe it . . . baby pigs. I have never seen anything so cute and so noisy all at the same time. They were Yorkshire pigs . . . pink as a party dress and bristly like little whisk brooms. Bob Pini said that they were 4-weeks-old and needed some mothering. One was smaller than the rest. I guess I was impulsive, but I don't regret it.

I took the runt. Mr. Pini tried to talk me out of her and Juan tried to talk me out of her. Mr. Pini said that if I wanted to raise a pig that could win at the County Fair I should look for strong legs, meaty shoulders and large hams. He expounded about a long pig with plenty of lean bacon and pork chops. He said that the runt was a bad specimen.

Juan told me that pigs were smart, very smart, and vocal and expressive. He shook his head and said, "You'll fall in love with that pig, and she will love you back. Don't do it, Syd."

While Mr. Pini and Juan debated the flavor versus the intelligence of pigs, I picked up Patty. That's her name, Sausage Patty. I picked her up and she didn't squeal. She kind of oinked and nuzzled me with her flat little snout. I think it was an oink. I have never heard an oink before but it was a cross between a snort, a burp and a grunt. It was so incredible. I scratched her head and she oinked louder and it got Mr. Pini's attention.

He started talking about "muscles in the ham region," and I asked, "How much is she?" He shook his head and said, "Girl, take her. That pig will be lucky to live the week . . . the runt is always trouble."

I doubt it. I really do. Getting a pig free just means that there will be more profit at the end of the project. We got out of there fast, before Pini changed his mind.

Right now, Patty is asleep in a cardboard box next to the bed. She looks like a china piggy bank in repose. She ate all of the leftovers from dinner: salad, sourdough rolls and fruit salad. Dad said we should call her Amana, after our garbage disposal. He scowled when I took her upstairs to my room, but I promised that tomorrow she would be moving into her pigpen. First I have to build it and develop a plan for her growth and development. I'm glad he didn't ask for any details. I don't know the first thing about raising a pig.

7

The Formula

Sunday, March 23

It is almost midnight! I am tired but too wired up to sleep. Juan and I hit the 4-H office, the library, the lumberyard and Pini's Mill again before noon.

I worked on the pen until dinner and on the winning market hog formula until almost 9 p.m. The 4-H literature says that a pig should weigh 200-240 pounds to be a fair contender. A healthy pig will gain from 1.5 to 1.8 pounds per day if fed properly. Wow!! There are 4 months or 120 days until the fair which runs from July 24 to August 1. A starter pig weighs about 50 pounds. Patty weighed in on the bathroom scale at 25 pounds, but we have a 2-week jump on most other kids, who won't get their pigs for another 14 days. Patty needs to gain 1.8 pounds a day to reach her ideal weight for the fair.

So her diet is important. The quality of food directly affects the size of the pig and the quality of the meat pigs produce. She will need different concentrations of nutrients and amounts of feed, depending on the stage of production. Harold Gribbs, the 4-H leader, sat down with me for an hour and laid out the road from pig to pork. Patty needs water, carbohydrates or fats for fattening, protein additives for building muscle, and minerals and vitamins to ensure good health.

It sounds complicated, but like Father says, the story is told by the bottom line. I can't believe I wrote that . . . quoting Father. But it looks like we can do it.

Formula for Raising a Winning Pig

Cost of Pig:	FREE
Cost of Equipment:	
Pigpen	$36 (for material; labor is free)
Hog Feeder	FREE (borrow from Meridas)
Water Barrel	FREE (borrow from Meridas)
Rubber Boots	10
Scrub Brush, Clippers, Cane	24
Cost of Feed:	84*
Miscellaneous Expenses:	
Fair Entry Fee	25
Veterinary Expense	50
Total Expenses	229
$2.50** x 241 lbs.	602.50
Less Expenses	<229.00>
PROFIT	$373.50

* 3.5 lbs. of feed per day x 120 days = 420 lbs.

** Price per lb. for winning pig

We built the pigpen. It was a lot of work but it was fun. Juan is an artisan—without his help, I could never have built the pen. It is more like a miniature barn or doghouse with a snug place for Patty to sleep and a small pasture for her to call home. Father helped for about a half hour, but his carpentry skills are limited, and we sent him in to do taxes. We had to rebuild his section of the fencing. Juan says that pigs are very strong, so a strong fence is critical. It's hard to believe watching little Patty explore her new home. After helping us all afternoon, she snorted around the fence perimeter, dug a hole in the middle of the pasture, and fell asleep in the wet dirt. We looked like pigs who had been sleeping in the dirt by the time we were through.

Juan stayed for dinner and then went home to write an essay for English class. I told him that mine was going to be entitled "To Market, to Market: The Intricacies of Pork Production in America at the End of the 20th Century," but, in fact, I think I will just hand in a piece I wrote for the school paper last week. A girl has limits . . . .

8

The Escape

Sunday, March 30

Patty weighed in tonight at 38.6 pounds! A pound above target, but there were added expenses.

Last night Juan and I went to the movies. The Night Lights Theater is an old warehouse outside of town that shows old movies on weekends. They were showing classic westerns, and we saw *Butch Cassidy and the Sundance Kid.* It's a pretty good movie. I have seen it before. Good thing, because I don't remember much. During the first train robbery scene Juan took my hand.

I have held hands before, and holding hands in the movies is like having popcorn and Raisinets. But there was something different about holding Juan's hand. I shivered. I think it was the shivers. My heart beat faster and even though I felt shivery, I felt warm at the same time. Later, on the way home, we held hands again. We talked about school, books, and the spring soccer league . . . anything but how close we felt.

We stopped off in the pigpen to say goodnight to Patty. She loves Juan. She snortles about and pushes him with her snout and begs to have her belly scratched.

Suddenly she threw herself at him and he fell into her food trough. I laughed so hard I leaned against the fence to catch my breath.

That is when Juan scrambled to his knees, pulled me into the trough, and kissed me. It was a real kiss and I got the shivers again. Juan said, "You are so wonderful when you laugh," and I said something stupid like "You are wonderful all the time." Then he said "I would have said that but I didn't want to overdo it," and then we both laughed and plopped down in the straw and played with Patty until Father turned the front porch lights on.

He turns the lights on at 10:00 p.m. because that's when I have to be home on weekends. I guess he doesn't want me to get lost in the dark.

Maybe it was the lights coming on or the kiss or just laughing but that is when I left the pigpen without securing the latch carefully. I guess that is what happened, because this morning when I got up, the gate was open and Patty was gone.

She wasn't gone for long. Before I could round up a posse and go look for her the telephone rang. It was Mrs. Benton who lives down the road. "There is a pig in my pantry and it looks suspiciously like the pig that I saw in your sideyard." She was talking to Father, but I could hear her from across the room. "This pig came through my dog door, terrified my poor Muffy, and ate an entire bag of premium dog kibble and a half bag of carrots and potatoes in the pantry. It has made a mess. It will not vacate."

"We will be right over, Mrs. Benton. Hold on!" said Father in fatherly tones.

"I think she is hyperventilating, Syd," he told me. " Let's go. Grab my wallet. This is going to cost you."

It did but it was worth it. Patty made a mess of Mrs. Benton's pantry. After she finished off the "quality kibble," she wanted the pies on the counter top but had to settle for the potatoes, carrots and turnips in the root bin. She is a messy eater, so the pantry looked like a dirty dinner plate.

We collected Patty, cleaned up and paid Mrs. Benton $10 for the food.

The amazing thing was that Father burst out laughing as soon as we got in the car. "Did you see the look on her face, Syd? I think it defines indignation."

I made the mistake of asking him if it was funny enough to be worth $10. It wasn't. All and all it was a fairly extraordinary weekend: Juan's kiss, father's laughter and Patty's extra pound, thanks to Mrs. Benton and Muffy.

9

Pigscapes

Monday, March 31

Patty's break-in was the talk of school today. I survived the jokes, including being charged as accessory to a prowling porker. Actually, in history Mr. Markert noted that during the Medieval Period, pigs were considered so intelligent that they were indicted and tried for crimes, like overrunning a neighbor's garden or knocking down a passerby. Remembering Juan's spill in the pigpen, I turned around to catch his eye, and he was already grinning. He whispered, "Thanks, Patty." I blushed and turned around quickly.

Today, for the first time, I felt like an insider instead of an outsider.

Wednesday, April 2

Got home late from the stables today and Patty was squealing for dinner. She was standing up on her hind hooves and kicking like a mule until it was served. I had an oatmeal cookie in my

pocket for dessert. When she finished the main course she backed me into a corner for that cookie. She has an amazing sense of smell! But her manners are not piggish at all!! I don't know why calling someone a pig is such an insult. She likes to eat all right, but she has manners. When she took the cookie from my hand, she smelled it first and then curled her lips over it and lifted it courteously. She chewed it thoroughly, and then smacked and licked her lips for almost a minute, savoring the sweetness. I think pigs are gourmets.

Gourmets with appetite!

Saturday, April 5

Juan came over this morning and we gave Patty a bath. She needs to get used to being hosed and scrubbed. She seemed to like it. Beans joined in, wrestling with the hose, and before we were through, we were all wet. Patty seems to like Beans. He knocks at her with his head and she butts him in return. Then they run in circles around the yard. I went inside to get towels for the wet people and when I came out Patty and Beans were wallowing in the mud hole that Patty has built in her pen. It was gross . . . the perfect pink pig and the brown and white dog were two muddy globs. Juan was laughing so hard, I was forced to turn the hose on all three of them.

Things got out of hand and there was a hose fight. There were no winners.

Sunday, April 6

I spent the morning at the stable. Jack was frisky. We worked on the three gaits: walk, trot and canter, and then Melissa, Carmel and I cleaned stalls. They pumped me for information about Juan

and me. I decided that Juan, above all things, was my best friend. I didn't want to put our friendship into the rumor mill, so I was "long on generalities and short on details." That is one of Father's expressions for my reports on the school day. It works.

In the afternoon, Juan, Beans, Patty and I went for a walk . . . all four of us. I never realized that pigs could be loyal or athletic. I started out with her on a leash, but by the end of the afternoon she was helping us pick wildflowers for Mrs. Merida. Actually, Patty was eating flowers. She seems to love evening primrose and cat's paws best. There were plenty, so we let her snack.

The seasons are so strange here. It is the first week of April. In New York we would be bracing for the last snowstorm of the season, just in time to ruin spring break. Here, the brown hills have turned into green hills spotted with the purple, orange and yellow of wildflowers. Strange but wonderful. It was also wonderful to lie close to Juan in the tall grass. We didn't talk about anything. We just lay there until Beans and Patty got bored and trampled us into playing pig tag.

Patty can run . . . she is faster than Beans. They ran across meadows and into shallow ponds formed by last week's rain. Water and mud are pig magnets.

Monday, April 7

Juan and I talked about us on the way home from school. We decided that our friendship was the most important thing, but being boyfriend and girlfriend was a close second. The best couples are those who really like each another and enjoy doing things together. Juan is easy to talk to . . . about school, about what comes after school, about Father, about Patty and Jack and Beans and movies and books and changes that turn your life upside-down and then back upright again. I feel upright again. We sealed our new relationship with a kiss.

I had dinner with the Merida's. The table's centerpiece was a huge soup pot full of yesterday's wildflowers because no vase was big enough. We talked about special effects in modern films and classic old black and white movies. Mr. Merida's favorite movie is *The Thin Man*, a 1930's mystery, and Mrs. Merida's favorite is *It Happened One Night*, a 1930's romantic comedy. Juan observed that some pretty good movies have been made in the last 60 years and that they should see *The Star Wars Trilogy*. He did the dishes for that particular observation. I helped.

Tuesday, April 8

Patty weighed in last night at 51.2 lbs. Right on target!! Her ears got sunburned yesterday. They were red and almost looked blistery. I called the vet, Dr. Langella, and he told me that pigs have very sun sensitive skin, which explains her love of mud and the shade. The mud cools her off and coats her pinkness so that she doesn't sunburn. She also has only a few sweat glands, so the cool mud is critical for regulating her body temperature.

I had to stop at the drugstore and get #30 sunblock. Apply 3 times a day to the tips of her ears. I have to add $10.95 to miscellaneous expenses.

10

Loss in Value

Tuesday, April 15

Patty is sick. I went out to feed her and she didn't come running to the bucket. She was lying in her bed and breathing funny. I coaxed her with an apple slice, a donut and a peanut butter sandwich, but she was not interested in eating at all. I rubbed her belly and wooed her with promises of fresh mud, but she just gasped and turned her head away. I called Mr. Gribbs at 4-H and he told me to call Dr. Langella right away. He said that it was serious when a pig would not eat and that I should not invest too much money because we could be looking at weight loss instead of weight gain.

I called Dr. Langella but he can't come until tomorrow morning. He has other animal emergencies.

Wednesday, April 16

No progress but a little hope.

When Dr. Langella arrived he gave Patty an examination . . . no appetite, listless, high temperature. He diagnosed acute pneumonia. It sounds awful . . . like a sentence rather than a diagnosis.

He said we caught it early and that she has a chance of recovery with a warm bed and a broad-spectrum antibiotic.

I got to school late and pretended I was sick so I could leave early. I got up last night to check on Patty, but Father caught me on the stairs and pointed me back to my bedroom. I didn't sleep so it doesn't make any sense to make me stay in bed.

Thursday, April 17

I told Father that I didn't feel well enough to go to school today. I am sure that he figured it out. I spent the day in the pen with Patty. She was so quiet, I could hold her and she didn't make a sound. I thought about what my friends back in New York would say if they could see me holding a sick pig and crooning "Patty cake, patty cake, baker man." There have been so many changes in the last few weeks. Sometimes I feel as if I am the one that is changing.

Friday, April 18

Patty ate.

Saturday, April 19

The week from hell is over. Patty is eating and squealing; signs of a healthy pig. Juan was great . . . especially with pilling the pig. Although she started eating yesterday, she wasn't her ravenous sweet self until this morning. I was so worried that I didn't go to the stables or school. She was so pitiful. She seemed to sense that I wanted to help her, and she barely objected when I took her temperature. I was the one who objected . . . taking a pig's temperature is another thing on my list of Don't Ever Want To Do Again.

Sunday, April 20

Bad News: Patty's weight gain was 3.8 pounds instead of 12.6. She weighs only 55 pounds, but she is healthy again. I know we can make up the lost weight now that she is eating. Of course, I have to subtract the veterinary bill of $50.00 and the $24.21 pharmacy bill for the antibiotics. Tomorrow, I am mixing some molasses and corn with her meals. This pig is going to gain weight.

Sunday, April 27

On target: Patty gained a phenomenal 2 lbs. a day this week and has added 14 lbs. to her growing middle. She weighs 69 lbs.

We had an informal riding competition at Tumbleweed yesterday. Jack and I took first place in the Novice Class. Juan was there. It felt good to do well. Later we went to a jazz concert at school. Juan knows a lot about music. He could name the composer of each piece without looking at the program. On the way home I hummed songs . . . classical and popular . . . and he knew every one. The evening ended badly, though. I told him about my 4-H assignment.

We have to go to supermarkets and other retail stores and identify 10 products that are made from the animal we are raising. The purpose of the assignment is to illustrate the value that each farm species plays in providing products for people. I went to the grocery store and found not only pork in the meat department, but also bologna, salami, sausage and hot dogs. I never knew that those meat products were made mostly from pigs. The butcher pointed out a big jar of pig's feet on the counter and I freaked.

Pig's feet!! Little feet with the cloven indentation . . . just like Patty's feet. I told Juan that it was hard for me to believe that people would eat pig's feet, that it made my skin crawl.

He asked me if I felt better eating salami or bologna because it didn't look like part of an animal. I told him that I didn't feel good eating salami, bologna, bacon or pork chops. Then he asked me how I could feed other people's appetite for pork with Patty.

I don't know why, but I started to cry and told him he was mean. I ran home. He called later and apologized. I know he didn't mean to make me miserable but I was and I am.

Saturday, May 3

Mr. and Mrs. Gribbs made me stay after the 4-H meeting today. Mr. Gribbs took the lead in telling me that my project looked like a value loss. He said that I have invested too much money in supplies and veterinary bills and supplements to Patty's diet to turn a significant profit. He said that he was also disturbed by my report on value.

In talking to the group about the importance of pigs to people, I just couldn't list pigskin jackets, salami, bologna and the worldwide importance of BLTs. I talked instead about how Patty had made me understand the intelligence of animals, especially animals that we don't keep as pets. I explained how sociable she was and how sensitive. I told the kids about how she stole Father's boots off the back steps and how she plays with Beans. Everybody laughed and I thought my talk went pretty well.

Mr. and Mrs. Gribbs did not think so. Mrs. Gribbs just shook her head a lot, while Mr. Gribbs told me that I was undermining the program by becoming emotionally involved with the project.

Patty will be slaughtered after the judging this summer and I have to prepare for that conclusion. "Can I simply enter Patty to win and the bring her home?" I asked.

"Young lady, the Fair is terminal. All animals entered are killed to prevent the spread of diseases that might result from contact with other animals at the event," Mr. Gribbs answered with that tone that adults use when they call kids know-it-alls.

Terminal . . . what an awful word. I don't know what to do.

Sunday, May 4

Patty gained her target weight.

I am over $100.00 in debt on the project. I don't have many alternatives but to go along with the 4-H guidelines.

11

Health to Better Living

Wednesday, May 7

Juan and I had lunch today. I brought up the pork issue. I told him that I will never eat anything made out of a pig ever again in my life. He asked me if I would eat Chicken Little and her offspring, the flock of chickens at his house. They have become some of my favorites at the Merida's. I knew where this conversation was going, but I didn't feel like avoiding it by crying or running away.

I told him he was right and I was the one who should have apologized last week.

I could toss and turn, hem and haw, rationalize, intellectualize, deliberate and contemplate, but the decision has made itself. I know it is a cow; I can't eat a drumstick and not know it is a chicken; and I can't eat sausage on a pizza and not know that it is Patty.

"The decision to be a vegetarian is really clear, but I don't know about being a vegan and not eating any animal products at all. Pizza is still pizza without pepperoni and sausage, but without cheese, it is just bread dipped in tomato sauce," I explained to Juan.

"Don't worry now about where you are going," Juan said gently. "Take some pride in how far you have come, and pack your own lunch tomorrow," he added as I passed on the cafeteria's beef burritos and ate one of his peanut butter and jelly sandwiches.

Thursday, May 8

I talked with Patty this morning over her breakfast. I did most of the talking, but she listened. You could tell. I told her about my library research on pigs. She liked the story about the pig near Houston, Texas that saved a drowning boy. The pig, named Priscilla, was out walking with the woman she lived with when she heard the cries of an 11-year old boy who had strayed too far from the shore while swimming in a lake. While onlookers watched in despair and then astonishment, Priscilla swam out to the boy and pulled him to safety as he held onto her leash.

I told her that if pigs could save people, I would save her. Just like I made a vow never to eat meat again, I promised Patty that I would see that she never became bologna. She looked up at me with a twitching snout and blinked twice. I decided that meant, "I am counting on you, Syd."

What am I going to do? I owe Father a small fortune. I started the whole thing with plans to become an equestrian phenomenon. I wanted Jack and I planned to sacrifice Patty to get him. Now I will do anything to save Patty. I don't think Father is going to be very receptive to begging. I have to come up with a plan.

Sunday, May 11

Patty is getting bigger. I stopped weighing her . . . . I guess I am hoping that she is a pygmy pig and will be too small for competition. Father asked for an accounting today. He was very enthusiastic about the prospects for a profit. He called it a "tidy sum." My debt is over $110!

Tuesday, May 13

I talked to some of the older 4-H kids at school. I was thinking that maybe I could get some ideas to save Patty. Sara Soomes, who won with a steer last summer, said that to be a winner you sometimes need help. She told me clenbuterol, a growth hormone, really beefs cattle up. It gives them the muscular physique of a champion.

I never heard of growth hormones. It was not a part of the 4-H informational package on animal rearing. Sara acted as if I was a dumb city slicker and said that a lot of kids use growth hormones because they really want to win.

What if I gave Patty hormones and she got too big?

Wednesday May 14

I stopped by Dr. Langella's clinic and asked about growth hormones. He was shocked. He told me these drugs are illegal and banned for use in the United States. I was shocked too. I wonder if Sara knows that they are illegal. Maybe she doesn't care. Dr. Langella said that some people only care about winning. Cheater or traitor? I guess what they're doing is no worse than selling a friend to slaughter.

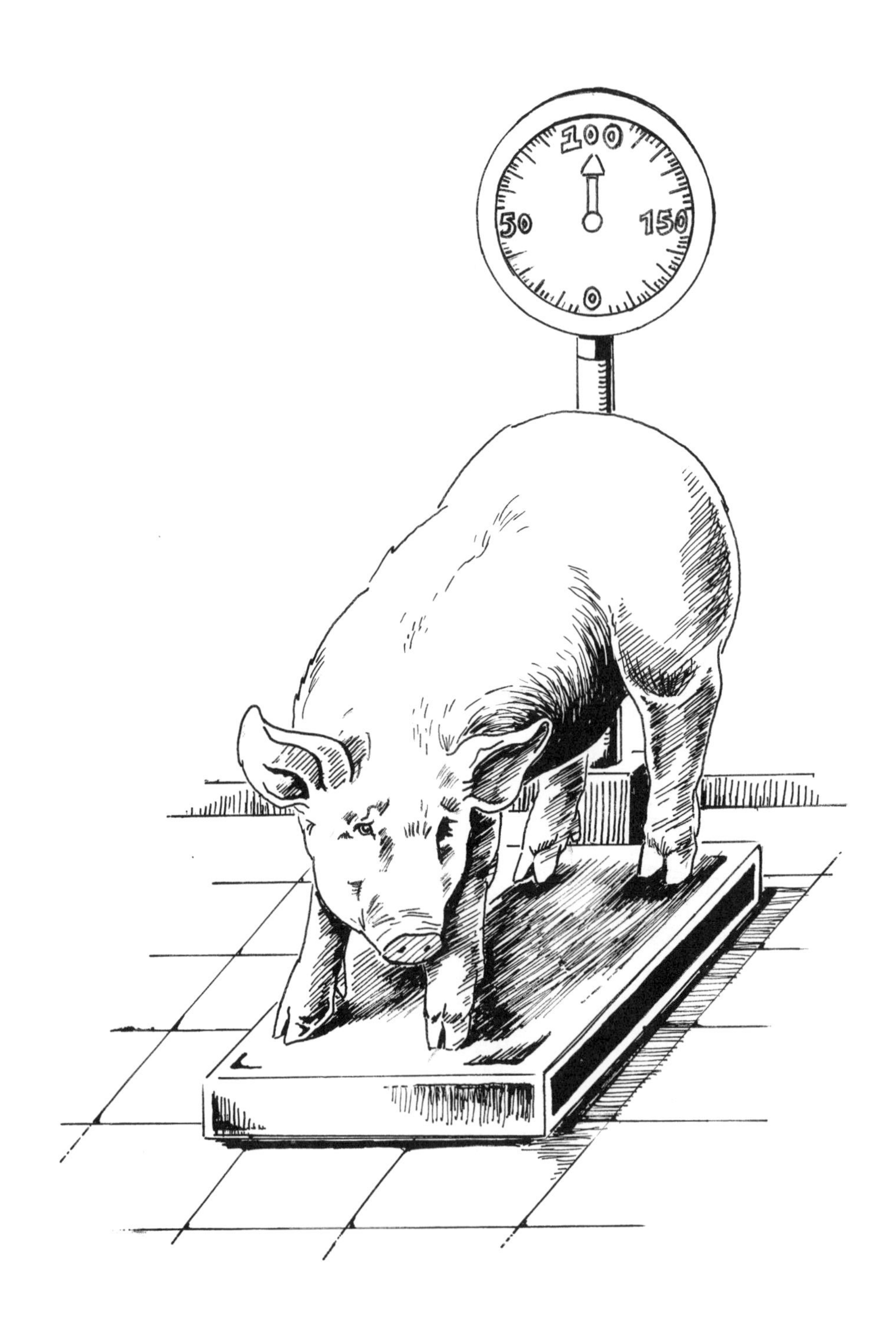
100
50
150
0

12

Heart to Greater Loyalty

Sunday, May 18

Patty weighs over 100 lbs! I tried to talk to Father about the project this afternoon, but he wanted to have another conversation. He told me that he was proud of the way I had managed the pig project so far and that his figures showed a nice profit even with the unexpected costs.

I tried to tell him that maybe, the project was a bad idea, that Patty was a person . . . well, not a person, but a pig individual and my friend . . . and that I wanted to abandon it. He looked down on me with his eyebrows forward for emphasis and said that he didn't want me to be a quitter. He said that the fact that something is difficult and requires me to set my feelings aside, is no reason to quit.

I didn't know what to say then, but I do now. Why should I set my feelings aside? Feelings are important. My feelings for Patty are important. My loyalty to her should come before stupid prize money.

Monday, May 19

Juan and I talked at lunch today. I told him that I had decided to choose loyalty to Patty over the prize money and my father's expectations and that I need his help.

He was wonderful. He told me that he has no idea what to do but that we will do something. He stressed the *we*.

We have to figure out a way to save Patty.

Thursday, May 23

No plan. I couldn't eat dinner last night. Father thinks it's because I am a reluctant vegetarian and I want a hamburger. It's just that I can't eat with Patty getting bigger by the day. She oinks at me as I come up the sidewalk from school as if to say, "So, what are we going to do?"

Monday, June 2

I have been too busy to write. The school year is winding down. We have final exams next week. Patty is getting bigger and Juan and I have gone through 100 different scenarios for her rescue.

Juan talked to his parents about giving Patty a home. They said that a 600 lb. full-grown pig is a difficult animal to care for and that they simply do not have the room. More importantly, even if the Meridas could take her, there is my father and his commitment to my commitment to the project. We tried to sort out some money making schemes to buy Patty out of the project, but it was a money making scheme that got us into this dilemma in the first place. If only she would run away somewhere safe. It's nobody's fault if the pig disappears.

Tuesday, June 3

We have it: a plan. Saturday, June 14 is the execution date. Not of Patty, of the plan. I am worried, but there is no choice. Patty is going to disappear right after final exams.

13

Head to Clearer Thinking

Sunday, June 15

God, confession is far better than capture.

Last night I met Juan at the pigpen at 4:30 a.m. Father is a light sleeper until near morning. We leashed Patty. She wasn't excited about getting up in the cold dark before dawn. I kept praying, "Please, do not squeal." A box of oatmeal cookies kept her quiet, and we walked down to an abandoned barn off Crawford Road, about 1/4 mile from the house.

We were about halfway there when we realized that we were being followed. A dark shadow seemed to be stalking us. Beans growled softly. "We see you!" I whispered into the gloom, and Juan shone the flashlight into Gus's face. Gus is our neighbor's Rottweiler. Beans' growls turned into a warning bark and Gus disappeared back into the night. Gus is harmless, but terror can kill. I could feel my heart banging against my chest.

We ducked into the barn just ahead of a Sonoma police patrol car. I could almost hear the police radio, "Two suspicious kids, a dog and a pig on Crawford Road. Send backup." We held our breath as the car purred softly by the old building and continued on toward the county line.

One box stall was in pretty good shape. Juan secured it with some old timber while I made Patty a straw bed. We had checked out the barn and set up everything we would need last week. I left two cookies for Patty, kissed Juan quickly and ran home to bed.

The hardest part came after breakfast. "Father, father," I yelled from the porch, "Patty is gone." I couldn't go in and face him. It was like lying. He calmly poured another cup of coffee and told me to start looking down at Mrs. Benton's. I ran down to the Crawford Road barn with Patty's breakfast instead.

The second hardest part was coming back to the house and telling Father that she wasn't at Mrs. Benton's and I couldn't find her. He told me to stay calm and post the neighborhood. "I hope that she hasn't been rustled," he mulled. "That pig was worth a penny plus. I want you to get on it, Syd. Call the police and Animal Control. A pig doesn't just disappear."

I pretended to go off and continue the search. I met Juan back at the barn.

"It isn't going to work, Juan," I moaned. "Father wants to call the police. We have to get the Humane Society out here right away to pick her up. Are you sure they can take care of her?"

Juan had called all the animal shelters the week before. He discovered that the Humane Society has facilities for farm animals, and they usually have no trouble finding a "pet" home for livestock. This means Patty will be a pal, not pork.

I didn't realize how awful . . . no, worse than awful . . . I was going to feel when the Humane Society trailer arrived at the barn.

Patty screamed and struggled when the two humane officers tried to load her in the trailer. She ran and cowered in one corner and bolted to another when they approached. It isn't easy to take a pig somewhere she does not want to go. Finally I put a leash around her neck and led her into the trailer. I starting sobbing when they slammed the trailer gate and she looked at me through the slats. I was losing Patty. To save Patty, I had to lose her.

I know now that rescuing Patty from the 4-H project was one thing, but losing Patty was another.

Juan and I wandered slowly back to the house. Father thought I was upset because I couldn't find Patty. I was a liar and a traitor.

Juan kept telling me that difficult circumstances require difficult responses, but I noticed that his eyes were wet. I took his hand and we were miserable together.

What we didn't know was that there was a witness.

Tuesday, June 17

Just after dinner the phone rang. Father picked it up. I heard him say, "Really . . . . Really . . . . Interesting . . . .Very interesting . . . . Not at all. Thank you, Mrs. Benton." He came into the kitchen where I was drying the dishes.

"Interesting. That was Mrs. Benton on the telephone. She said she saw some shadowy figures including one shaped like a pig pass her house before dawn on Sunday morning.The other figures looked like a boy, a girl and a dog. She says she also saw a Humane Society truck and trailer out at the old Crawford barn later that day and heard some awful squealing. She wanted to know if that pig of ours was in trouble again."

When Father said, "Syd, tomorrow I will be home early and you and I are going for a little ride," I knew I was busted.

I sputtered twice and Father said, "Syd, I don't think you should say anything. Go to your room."

I know an order when I hear one. I can live with disappointing Father, but not with disappointing Father and Patty.

14

Hands to Larger Service

Wednesday, June 18

We rode silently to the Humane Society shelter. We got there just before it closed, but Patty wasn't there. A nice woman at the front desk confirmed my father's suspicions and doomed my fate. She told him that Patty had been picked up by officers at the barn on Crawford Road after being reported by a Mr. Juan Merida. She had been brought to the shelter late on Sunday but was so lethargic and apparently depressed that she had been transferred to Animal Place the following day.

I had many questions, but Father made it clear that I was not entitled to speak.

The woman gave us directions to Animal Place: down the highway, a gravel road to the left, a dirt road to the right, through two gates to a green valley surrounded by oak trees.

I saw Patty right away. No, it wasn't Patty. It was another pig. There was Patty. No that pig was much bigger than Patty . . . huge in fact. As we parked in front of a long log building, I realized that the fenced meadow was full of pigs, cows and goats.

I heard Patty before I saw her. She was in a smaller pasture near the log building with two other young pigs. She came running and squealing. She felt like I did. I leaped the low fence and ran to my friend. We both cried. I think pigs cry. OK, I was sobbing. It didn't matter that Father was mad or that he could see me crying. Nothing mattered but Patty.

I don't remember much that happened then, except that a woman came from the building and talked to Father while I clutched snortling Patty. Father finally came over and kind of picked me up. He said, "Syd, sometimes I can be oblivious, but not all the time. It doesn't excuse your lying and deception, but it does explain it. You are more like your mother than you are like me and that is a good thing."

It was amazing, but not as amazing as what happened next. Father started to cry, really cry, and we hugged and cried until the Animal Place woman coughed politely.

Thursday, June 19

Juan came over tonight to apologize to Father. They shook hands. It was very grown-up. No lectures. No warnings.

I had so much to tell Juan. We sat in Patty's pen and I told him about Animal Place, a safe sanctuary for farm animals who were rescued from roadways, auctions, slaughterhouses and 4-H projects. I told him that I wasn't going to be taking riding lessons anymore or going to 4-H meetings. I was going to Animal Place every Saturday. I had to put in 4 hours a week cleaning stalls, hauling feed and grooming animals as a contribution for Patty's care. She will be safe in the company of other pigs there for her whole life. I can see her and be her friend and she can be a pig. I told him that I figured I had completed my 4-H project, because I had learned to think with my head about the loyalties of the heart and that my hands were going to be kept busy in service that made me feel healthier and happier than I had in a long time.

"That's 5 H's, not 4," Juan commented, "Happiness isn't a part of the program."

"But happiness is a part of the new 5-H program," I offered with a grin. "Orphaned baby animals, piglets, lambs, and calves often end up at livestock auctions, which are just halfway houses to the meat counter. I was thinking that we could go over to the auction in Petaluma after school on Tuesday and rescue two lambs and raise them here in Patty's pen. With a little renovation this pig pen could be transformed into a sheep shed and we could . . . ."

I didn't get to finish my proposal because Juan vaulted the pen fence, laughing as he ran down the road toward home with Beans at his heels. Tomorrow I am going to work on the details and make a more convincing presentation.

ANIMAL PLACE

Few readers may actually ever face the dilemma raised in this story, but all of us are part of a system that sees pigs, cows, sheep and goats as sausage patties, hamburgers and lamb chops.

Contact Animal Place for more information on how you can protect animals like Patty. Animal Place is a nonprofit sanctuary started in 1989. It cares for abused and unwanted 'farm' animals, such as pigs, sheep, cattle, goats, chickens and others. All have a special story. Some were rescued from auction yards, some from factory farms, and others from research laboratories.

Animal Place
3448 Laguna Creek Trail
Vacaville, CA 95688
(707) 449-4814 Fax (707) 449-8775
E-Mail: Porcilina@aol.com
Home Page:
http://envirolink.org/arrs/animal_place/ap_www.htm

A few introductions of those living at Animal Place

Penelope was brought to Animal Place by a young girl who did not want to see her killed and eaten.

Jesse was rescued by Farm Santuary as a young calf after she jumped out of a truck that was taking her to auction in Colorado. She suffered severe injuries during the escape but healed beautifully.

Mary was rescued from the California State Fair where she was born. Her mother was on display so fairgoers could see a sow give birth. Mary was the runt of the litter.

Betty was a hen used for research. She had never been outside a cage. After arriving at Animal Place, however, she soon learned to scratch the earth for seeds and take dust baths.

Joe was left to die on top of a "dead pile" at an auction yard in Oregon.

About the Author . . .

Diane Allevato has been involved in animal protection work for 25 years. She has three border collies and a cat, but no pig although she appreciates them greatly.

About the Illustrator . . .

Trish Van den Bergh is an 18-year-old vegan studying cartooning at the School of Visual Arts.